AL RODIN

LITTLE
ECHO

tundra

Have you ever heard an Echo?

Maybe you have.
They live in lakes
and tunnels
and caves.

But have you ever seen
an Echo?

Little Echo was a very shy Echo.

She spent her days hiding
and sneaking
and searching
for sounds . . .

Whenever she heard the other beasts playing and laughing and making big **TAWOOs,** she longed to join in.

Yet all she could do was hide and echo from the shadows.

Nobody ever knew
she was there.

Then one day, Max arrived.
"I am here to find the **Treasure!**"
Max announced to the cave.

Little Echo liked the sound of Treasure!

So she decided to **sneak** behind Max for a little while . . .

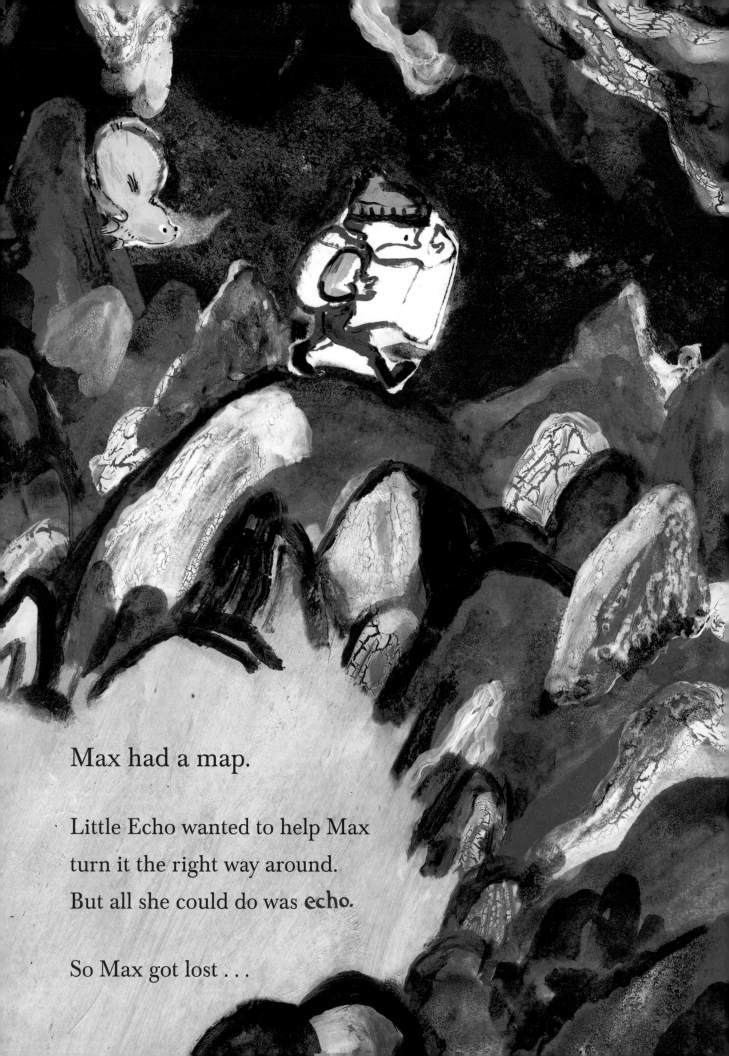

Max had a map.

Little Echo wanted to help Max
turn it the right way around.
But all she could do was echo.

So Max got lost . . .

Max had a shovel.

Little Echo wanted to show Max
the best spots for digging.
But all she could do was echo.

So Max hit lots of rock . . .

Max had a plan!

"I will not leave this cave until I find the Treasure!" said Max.

Little Echo wanted to tell Max that he was in Bear's sleeping spot.

But she was too scared. She couldn't even echo.

And then
        Bear came back . . .

And Bear was angry.

And Bear was hungry.

And Max was fast asleep.

So Little Echo gulped twice and pinched herself to be brave,
and for the first time in her life she got ready to say
her very own words . . .

"RUN!"

shouted Little Echo.

RUN!

RUN!

RUN!

UN!

UN

UN

UN

UN

UN

UN

UN

UN

N

N

So Max ran.

And Little Echo ran too!

They hid until the coast was clear.
"You saved me!" said Max. "When I find
this Treasure, I'll give half of it to you!"

But Little Echo didn't want Max to leave
without her. She didn't want to go back
to the shadows.

So Little Echo gulped twice and pinched
herself to be brave, and for the second time
in her life she said her very own words . . .

"Could I look for the Treasure with you?" *ou*

said Little Echo. Her voice grew from a whisper.

"I have lots of ideas about where it might be." *ee ee*

ee

Max looked at Little Echo.

Little Echo looked at Max.

"All right," said Max.
"But I should warn you —
my map doesn't work."

Little Echo turned Max's
map the right way
around and off
they went.

As they searched, Max hummed.

As Max hummed, Little Echo echoed.

So Max echoed too.

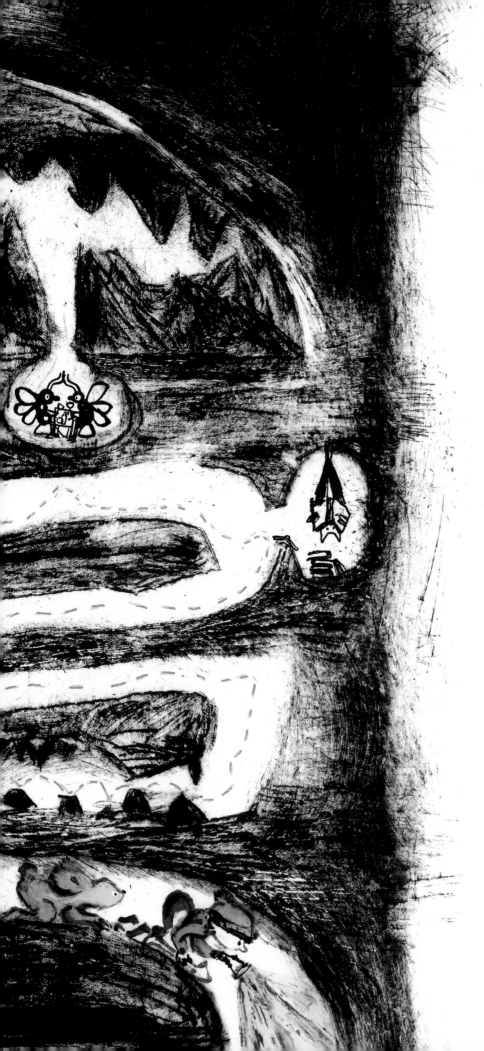

Together they
picked a spot
and drew a big

X.

And when they
were ready they

DUG

and

DUG

and

DUG.

Until
finally
they found . . .

... NOTHING.

"Maybe there really is no Treasure," said Little Echo.

This was a very disappointing thought.
A TERRIBLE and disappointing thought.

"Do you want to play something else?" said Max.
"How about **PIRATES?**" said Little Echo.
"I'll be the captain," said Max.
"And I'll be in charge!" said Little Echo.

So Little Echo and Max played
pirates. They ate marshmallows.
And stole a ship. And sailed off
to smuggle things.

And Little Echo started to tell
Max the secret things she had
always wanted to say.

As Little Echo talked,
Max listened.
As Little Echo listened,
Max talked too.

And they were having such a
good time listening and talking,
and talking and listening that
they forgot all about . . .

. . . the
Treasure.

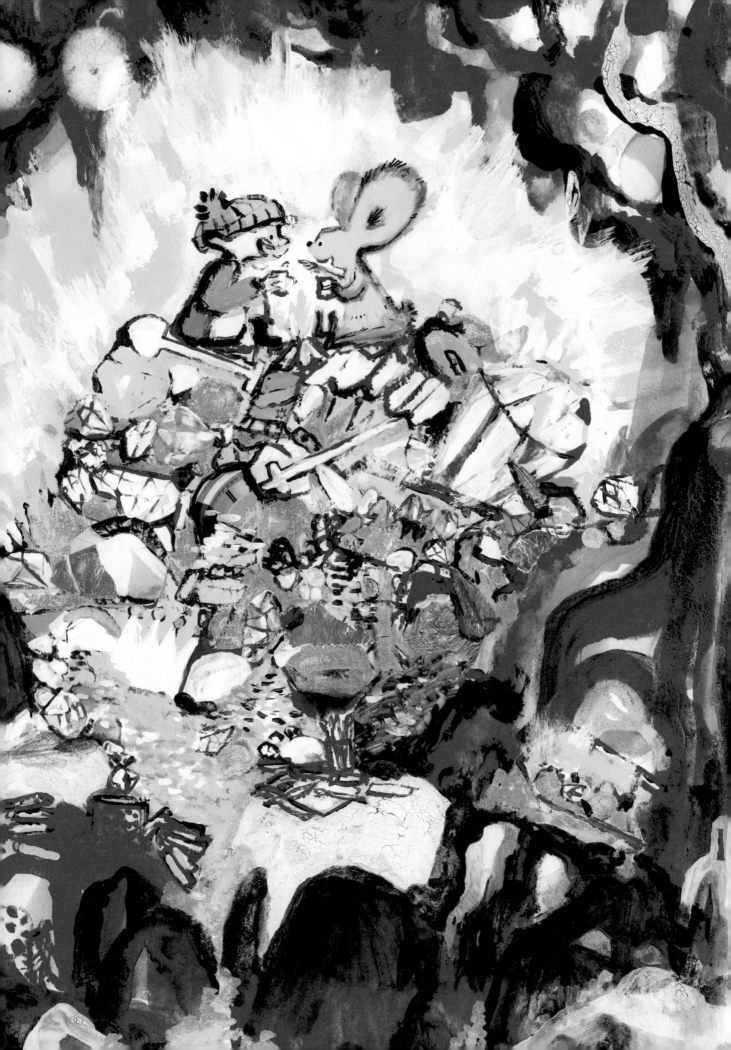

For Kate

First published by Puffin Books, 2021
Published in hardcover by Tundra Books, 2022

Tundra Books, an imprint of Tundra Book Group, a division of
Penguin Random House of Canada Limited

Library and Archives Canada Cataloguing in Publication

Title: Little Echo / written and illustrated by Al Rodin.
Names: Rodin, Al, author, illustrator.
Description: Previously published: London: Puffin Books, 2021.
Identifiers: Canadiana (print) 2021034606X | Canadiana (ebook) 20210346078 |
ISBN 9781774880623 (hardcover) | ISBN 9781774880630 (EPUB)
Classification: LCC PZ7.1.R65 Lit 2022 | DDC j823/.92—dc23

Published simultaneously in the United States of America by Tundra Books of Northern New York, an
imprint of Tundra Book Group, a division of Penguin Random House of Canada Limited

Library of Congress Control Number: 2021948740

Printed in China

1 2 3 4 5   26 25 24 23 22

www.penguinrandomhouse.ca